THE HOUSE
GOBBALEEN

• • •

THE HOUSE GOBBALEEN

• • •

by **Lloyd Alexander**

illustrated by **Diane Goode**

DUTTON CHILDREN'S BOOKS
NEW YORK

Library of Congress Cataloging-in-Publication Data

Alexander, Lloyd.
The House Gobbaleen/by Lloyd Alexander
illustrated by Diane Goode. — 1st ed.
p. cm.
Summary: Unhappy over what he considers his bad luck,
Tooley ignores his cat's warnings and invites a greedy little man
into his home in the mistaken hope
of improving his fortunes.
ISBN 0-525-45289-3
[1. Luck — Fiction. 2. Cats — Fiction.]
I. Goode, Diane, ill. II. Title.
PZ7.A3774Ho 1995
[Fic] — dc20 93-23300 CIP AC

Published in the United States 1995 by Dutton Children's Books,
a division of Penguin Books USA Inc.
375 Hudson Street, New York, New York 10014
Designed by Sara Reynolds
Printed in Hong Kong
First Edition
1 3 5 7 9 10 8 6 4 2

FOR THOSE WHO ARE LUCKY
WITHOUT KNOWING IT

L.A.

◆ ◆ ◆

FOR PETER

D.G.

NCE THERE WAS
a fellow named Tooley, always grumbling about his bad luck. Either his potatoes grew small, or his roof leaked, or his pig broke out of her sty and rooted up his cabbages. He was sure he was the unluckiest person in the world.

Tooley kept a long-legged yellow cat named Gladsake, and whenever his master fumed and fretted, Gladsake did his best to set him straight.

"Now listen to me, Tooley," said the cat. "Which would you rather have? Small potatoes or none? A roof with a leak or a leak without a roof? It's the nature of a pig to break out of a sty, as it's the nature of a sty to be broken out of. Your luck's no better nor worse than anyone else's. So let it be, and go about your business."

◆ ◆ ◆

◆ ◆ ◆

But Tooley would have none of that. "No, no, it's luck I need. The Friendly Folk have it. If only I could lay hold of one of them, that's when you'd see things look up."

So he began, each night, setting a basin of milk and some bread and cheese on his doorstep to draw one of the Friendly Folk. But first, along came a thunderstorm and curdled the milk. Then a crow flew down and made off with the bread and cheese. At last, he put out a jug of cider and a kipper, for all Gladsake's telling him it was a waste of good food and drink.

And sure enough, next morning when Tooley opened his door, there was a round-bellied, round-cheeked little man in a green leather jacket, tucking into the kipper and washing it down with the cider as fast as he could swallow.

"Here's the luck come at last!" shouted Tooley. "Oh, your honor, am I glad to see you. I can just feel the luck stirring already."

◆ ◆ ◆

"Stir, is it?" said the fat little creature, sucking a tooth. "Go stir me some porridge, and put a nice lump of butter in it."

"Two lumps!" cried Tooley. "Come into the house, your honor. Put yourself at ease, for my luck's been that bad you'll need all your strength to turn it around."

"Hooks is my name," said the little man. "Do you ask me in? For I've got to tell you this, Tooley: Once in, never out; and once out, never back."

◆ ◆ ◆

"If you want my advice, Tooley," muttered Gladsake, "I'd say give him his porridge and send him on his way. He's got a lopsided, squinny-eyed look to him I don't care for at all."

"Hush, you foolish cat," whispered Tooley, "and don't go judging your betters. He's one of the Friendly Folk, that's plain to see."

"There's good and bad among them," replied the cat, "and he looks like riffraff to me."

Paying no mind to Gladsake, Tooley urged his guest inside.

Once across the threshold, Hooks looked around and nodded.

"It's a snug little place you have, Tooley," said he. And he plumped himself into Tooley's favorite chair and settled himself as comfortably as if it had been his own. Then he pulled a clay pipe from his jacket and demanded tobacco to fill it.

While Gladsake, still muttering disapproval, rummaged out a jar of tobacco, Tooley hurried to the kitchen for a bowl of porridge.

◆ ◆ ◆

When he came back, there was Hooks puffing away and making a dreadful stink. Even so, sure his luck would be worth the stench, Tooley cheerfully handed over the porridge.

Hooks downed it in one gulp and smacked his lips. He stuffed his pipe again and folded his hands over his paunch, which seemed to have grown rounder within the instant.

"That's right, your honor," said Tooley, "enjoy yourself and take your rest. Oh, I can see it: You're gathering yourself up for all the luck you mean to bring me."

"Me bring you luck?" answered Hooks. "It's you bring me some drink."

No sooner had Tooley fetched another jug of cider than Hooks drank it off and called for more. And for the rest of the day, Tooley had not so much as a minute to mind his own chores. Hooks kept him on the go, first bringing a pillow to put behind his head, then a stool to put under his feet, then a kettle of tea, then a plate of seedcakes, until Tooley came to be as

◆ ◆ ◆

weary as if he had done the hardest day's work of his life. But, even though his feet ached from running back and forth at Hooks's beck and call, his spirits only brightened.

"After all this," he said, "I know your honor has something big in store for me. You needn't tell anything ahead of time. Only just give a little bit of a nod if I'm on to it. The biggest of all, isn't it? The pot of gold!"

◆ ◆ ◆

◆ ◆ ◆

"Pot of gold?" snapped Hooks. "Pot of stew! And let's have it now, Tooley, with a few dumplings to settle my digestion."

Trying his best to choke down his impatience, Tooley did as he was told, sure his grand surprise would follow. But Hooks, having polished off the whole pot of stew, leaving Tooley and Gladsake to chew on the gristle, heaved himself out of the chair.

"It's time!" cried Tooley. "It's coming now!"

"Time for bed," grunted Hooks.

And without so much as a good night, he waddled into Tooley's bed chamber, climbed into Tooley's bed, pulled Tooley's quilt over his head, and fell sound asleep that instant, snoring loud enough to shake the roof.

"The dear soul, he must be fairly worn out getting the luck ready for me," declared Tooley, swallowing his disappointment. "You'll see, my fine cat, what the morning brings."

Tooley spent a restless night on some straw on the floor.

◆ ◆ ◆

Next morning, instead of Hooks bringing him luck, it was
Tooley brought his guest breakfast in bed. And the rest of the
day passed like the one before, with Hooks planted in Tooley's
chair, bawling for bacon, kippers, more jugs of cider; scooping
fistfuls of tobacco from the jar; and puffing such clouds of

❖ ❖ ❖

smoke that Gladsake could hardly stop coughing and sneezing.

And so it went the following day, and the day after that. The only difference was that Hooks kept getting fatter and fatter, until he was round as a pumpkin and more demanding than ever.

❖ ❖ ❖

◆ ◆ ◆

Now, Tooley was by no means the quickest-witted fellow in the world. But seeing his larder grow barer by the hour, and himself turned out of his own chair and chamber, he began thinking how his luck was a little slow in coming.

At last he ventured, "Begging pardon, your honor, as I know you're saving yourself for something grand in the way of my luck, but I wonder if you couldn't spare a bit of it now, as you might say, on account."

"What luck?" retorted Hooks. "I promised you no luck. Be off, man. Fetch more drink, as the pot's near empty."

"No luck?" cried Tooley. "Then save us and spare us, but what am I doing waiting on you hand and foot? And gobbled out of house and home! With never a decent night's sleep in my own bed! And no luck at the end of it!"

"Once in, never out. That's what I said," answered Hooks. "You'd best keep on doing as I tell you, or you'll surely wish you had."

◆ ◆ ◆

As soon as Tooley had everything ready, Gladsake gave a yowl of terror and sprang onto the lap of the drowsing Hooks.

"Get off, you great lubber!" cried Hooks, while Gladsake clung to him as though for dear life. "What are you up to?"

"Nothing, your honor," Gladsake replied. "I didn't see him. No, no, not even a glimpse."

"Eh?" said Hooks. "Didn't see what?"

"I didn't see a House Gobbaleen," said Gladsake.

"House Gobbaleen?" retorted Hooks. "I never heard of one. There's no such thing."

◆ ◆ ◆

"Of course not," Gladsake hastily agreed. No sooner had he said this than, spitting madly, he sprang to the floor.

"What is it?" cried Hooks.

"Didn't you see him, then?" asked Gladsake. "Didn't you see those eyes big as saucers? Teeth sharp as pitchforks?"

"I saw nothing at all," snapped Hooks.

"Ah, well, then," said Gladsake, "neither did I."

Hooks snorted angrily. Nevertheless, he glanced uneasily around. And, for the rest of the day, whenever Hooks was comfortably settled, Gladsake would skitter about the room with his back arched and his tail like a bottlebrush, all the while assuring his guest that the Gobbaleen was not lurking under the table or behind the door or up the chimney.

◆ ◆ ◆

"Pay the cat no mind, your honor," said Tooley. "You know what daft creatures they are. There's no House Gobbaleen here at all, and that's the pure truth."

"You're up to no good," burst out Hooks. "When a fellow starts talking of pure truth, be sure there's a lie in it somewhere."

"It's true, nevertheless," put in Gladsake. "There's no such thing as a Gobbaleen. You said so yourself."

"Then why keep telling me?" retorted Hooks, squinting shrewdly at the cat. "Unless there is and you'd have me think there isn't."

"Unless there isn't and I'd have you think there is," replied Gladsake. "There might be a Gobbaleen I didn't want you to know about. But in that case, I might say there was and have you think there wasn't. Unless, of course, there was one. But there's none at all, as I've been telling you."

"Stop!" shouted the befuddled Hooks, shaking his fist at Gladsake. "You're hiding something from me. When I find it out, so much the worse for you."

◆ ◆ ◆

◆ ◆ ◆

With that, he stumped off to Tooley's bed. Next morning, when he came for his breakfast, his eyes were baggy, his lumpy nose trembled, and he kept looking anxiously over his shoulder.

"Good morning, your honor," said Gladsake. "You seem a little peaky. Didn't you sleep well?"

"Never a wink," snapped Hooks. "There was something sharp as brambles jabbing and pinching, scratching and tweaking at me every time I moved."

"It couldn't have been the Gobbaleen crept into the mattress," said the cat, "as there's no such thing. But if there was, that's just what he'd do."

"Don't start up again," cried Hooks, his voice quavering. "Tell your master to hurry some food and drink on the table."

So saying, to calm himself he loaded his pipe from the tobacco jar, lit up, and began puffing furiously. A moment later, his face went green; he coughed and grimaced and flung away the pipe as if it had bitten him.

"Stench and stagnation! This tobacco might as well be moldy cabbage!"

"It's no fault of the Gobbaleen," Gladsake assured him. "No, that couldn't be."

◆ ◆ ◆

◆ ◆ ◆

"Oh, couldn't it?" Hooks retorted. "The more you tell me it isn't, the more I know it is. You've got some nasty creature here. It's the same one bedeviled me all night. And you dare tell me that's not so?"

And with that, he seized the pot of cider Gladsake had brought and pegged it down in one gulp. Then his eyes began watering, he clutched his throat and pounded his heels on the floor. He spat and sputtered and dashed the pot to the ground.

"What's got into the drink?" he gasped. "Sour as vinegar! That's the Gobbaleen's doing, and never you try pretending it isn't."

"Even if it was," replied Gladsake, "your honor wouldn't be afraid of him, for all his teeth and claws. You're one of the Friendly Folk. You'd know how to deal with him."

"Not my line of work," muttered Hooks uneasily.

While Hooks peered under the chair and squinted anxiously into the corners and up the chimney, Gladsake went into the kitchen, where Tooley was waiting for him.

◆ ◆ ◆

◆ ◆ ◆

"Come on, now," ordered the cat. "Get about the rest of our business. He has that Gobbaleen stuck in his head like a burr. Quick, take him his breakfast as I told you."

A moment later, Tooley hustled in with the iron pot and set it on the table. "There, your honor," he said. "Eat hearty. Today's the day some good thing's bound to happen."

Hooks only grunted and, for the first time, showed no sign of appetite. His eyes darted around the room; he sat hunched in his chair, fidgeting his fingers and muttering to himself. Tooley, however, kept urging him to eat and, at last, snatched the lid from the pot.

◆ ◆ ◆

◆ ◆ ◆

Gladsake, coiled inside, burst out like a jack-in-the-box, teeth bared and eyes blazing. Bristling until he looked three times his size, yowling at the top of his voice, he shot into the air so quickly that he seemed a bolt of yellow lightning.

"It's himself!" squealed Hooks. "T H E   G O B B A L E E N!"

Shrieking in terror, he leaped off the chair, overturning the table in his efforts to flee the monstrous Gobbaleen. As crockery shattered around him, Hooks lost his footing and pitched to the floor. But he had grown so round and fat on Tooley's hospitality that he could not pick himself up again. Instead, arms and legs flailing, he went rolling like a cannonball, faster every moment.

Seeing his plan work better than he could have hoped, Gladsake was nimble enough to spring in front of the careening Hooks. He flung open the door. Without slackening speed, the whirling figure shot across the threshold.

"Once in, never out!" cried Gladsake. "Once out, never back! Good-bye, farewell, your honor. Keep an eye peeled for the Gobbaleen."

But Hooks heard none of that as he kept rolling through the dooryard, over the field, and down the hill until he vanished from sight.

From then on, though nothing went better or worse than it had before, Tooley never again complained of his luck.

◆ ◆ ◆